Hi, I'm **Carrie**

And I'm D...

Welcome to our **Jump Up** and **Join In** series.

We hope you enjoy reading the books and joining in with the songs.

This book is called **Lion's Speedy Sauce**.

I love this one, it's about **rhythm** and counting.

Yeah, it's a good one, remember to **turn the page** when you hear this sound . . . .

ROAR!

EGMONT

We bring stories to life

First published in Great Britain 2013
by Egmont UK Limited,
The Yellow Building, 1 Nicholas Road, London W11 4AN
www.egmont.co.uk

Text copyright © Carrie and David Grant 2013
Illustrations copyright © Ailie Busby 2013

Carrie and David Grant and Ailie Busby have asserted their moral rights

ISBN 978 1 4052 5833 3

A CIP catalogue record for this title is available from the British Library

Stay safe online.
Egmont is not responsible for content hosted by third parties.

Please note:
Adult supervision is
recommended when
scissors are in use.

For
Olivia, Talia,
Imogen and Nathan
– Carrie and David –

For Ruby x
– Ailie –

EGMONT LUCKY COIN

Our story began over a century ago, when seventeen-year-old
Egmont Harald Petersen found a coin in the street.

He was on his way to buy a flyswatter, a small hand-operated
printing machine that he then set up in his tiny apartment.

The coin brought him such good luck that today Egmont has
offices in over 30 countries around the world. And that lucky
coin is still kept at the company's head offices in Denmark.

Carrie and David Grant

Lion's Speedy Sauce

Illustrations by Ailie Busby

Remember to turn the page when the lion **roars!**

EGMONT

Lion's band was practising for an important concert at the Summer Fair.

But the sun was shining so brightly that Lion began to feel a little bit sleepy . . .

"One . . .

two . . .

And the band began to march s l o w e r . . .

and slower...

and slower...

The band decided to buy Lion
a clock to help him
keep time . . .

tick-tock

tick-tock

but the tick-tock, tick-tock
seemed to make Lion even sleepier!

"Phew," gasped the band, who had almost fallen asleep too.

Lunch
was Lion's
favourite
curry!

. . . the band added a little bit more!

After such a spicy lunch Lion felt wide awake.
He beat his bongos **in time**.

"One,

two,

one,

two!"

The band marched into town to play at the Summer Fair and thanks to Lion's spicy, speedy sauce . . .

. . . they were a
roaring success!

Lion's Speedy Sauce sing-along song

Attention!

It's really a waste,
We're losing the race,
My marching band
Can't find the pace.
I say to go slow,
I say to go quick,
My speedy sauce might do the trick
(here we go).

Chorus:
Left, right, left, right, keep the pace,
Marching up and down
(come on, come on).
Left, right, left, right, our parade
Is marching into town.

Look sharp.
Hey!
Come on.
That's better.

Can this really be,
That suddenly
My soldiers march along with me.
I say to go slow,
I say to go quick,
My speedy sauce has done the trick
(come on now).

Chorus:
Left, right, left, right, keep the pace,
Marching up and down
(you're looking good now).
Left, right, left, right, our parade
Is marching into town (step it up x 4).

Woo!
Come on.
Are you ready?
All together now!

Left, right, left, right,
Keep it up, keep it up.
Left, right, left, right,
Speed it up, speed it up.
Left, right, left, right,
Keep it up, keep it up.
Left, right, left, right,
Come on, let's go!

Oh oh oh, oh oh oh, oh oh oh, oh,
Keep it going now.
Oh oh oh, oh oh oh, oh oh oh, oh,
Keep it up, keep it up, keep it up.

Chorus:
Left, right, left, right, keep the pace,
Marching up and down.
(Boom, boom, boom, boom, boom!)
Left, right, left, right, our parade
Is marching into town.

Oh oh oh, oh oh oh, oh oh oh, oh,
Look left, look right.
Oh oh oh (come on), oh oh oh (come on),
oh oh oh, oh,
Keep it up, keep it up, keep it up now.

Chorus x 3

Attention!

When you play Track **7**, the karaoke track, sing along
to the whole song! Your special solo parts are in **bold**.

Clever Clapping on the Beat

This story was all about **rhythm**.

Rhythm helps music to flow and keeping **in time** is a great thing to practise.

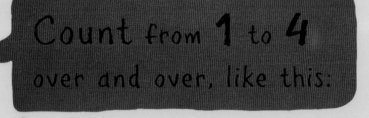

Count from **1** to **4** over and over, like this:

1   2   3   4   1   2   3   4

Now try **clapping** every time you say **1** and **3**, like this:

1   2   **3**   4   **1**   2   **3**   4

Now you can swap over numbers and clap every time you say **2** and **4**, like this:

1 **2** ₃ **4** 1 **2** ₃ **4**

Now, if there are **two** of you, one can clap on the **1** and **3** and the other on the **2** and **4**, like this:

1 **2** **3** **4** **1** **2** **3** **4**

For our **Jump Up and Join In** series we really want to get children interested in music and how it works. It shouldn't have to be rocket science and we want to encourage you as a parent, teacher or carer to teach your children with confidence. If you can learn it then you can pass it on.

Track 6 ## Super Scales on the Stairs

In this book we're going to start with **scales**. Look at the picture of the stairs. Let's think about our voices climbing up the stairs . . .

4
(Fa)

3
(Mi)

2
(Re)

lowest

1
(Do)

Make your own Bangin' Bongos!

You'll need:

Two saucepans*   Greaseproof paper   Big elastic bands
Sellotape   Wide ribbon   Pencil   Scissors

* You can also make the bongos with flowerpots or empty rubbish bins.

Step 1 Put the saucepans upside down on top of the greaseproof paper. Draw around the rims of both pans with a pencil.

Cut out two big circles, slightly bigger than the pencil circles you have just drawn.

Step 2 Fix a circle around the rim of each saucepan with the elastic bands and secure with sellotape.

Make sure the paper is pulled very tightly around the rim of each pan.

Step 3 Wrap the wide ribbon underneath the rim of each saucepan to cover up the elastic and the sellotape.

Tie in a bow around the handle.

Step 4 Now bang those bongos and keep a steady beat, just like Lion!

About Carrie and David

Carrie and David are best known for their hugely successful CBeebies series, **Carrie and David's Popshop**. They have coached Take That, The Saturdays and The Spice Girls and have a top-selling vocal coaching book and DVD. In 2008 they were awarded a BASCA for their lifetime services to the music industry.

Parents to four children, Carrie and David are passionate about getting all children to sing and are keen to encourage adults to feel more confident in teaching their little ones music skills from an early age. The **Jump Up And Join In** series was born as a result of this passion and will help young children learn a set of basic skills and develop a real love of music. As ambassadors for **Sing Up** – a not-for-profit organisation providing the complete singing solution for schools – and judges of the young singers on BBC 1's **Comic Relief Does Glee Club**, Carrie and David believe children everywhere should be given the tools to enjoy, and to feel confident about, practising music in all its shapes and forms.

Thanks for jumping up
and joining in!
Till the next time, bye!